TALES FROM

LAMPLIGHT LANE

Book 2

THE ASTEROID OF PROBABLE DOOM

Darren S. Philibert

Whimsical Publications, LLC

Florida

To purchase the authorized electronic edition of
Tales from Lamplight Lane: The Asteroid of Probable Doom, visit
www.whimsicalpublications.com

Cover art by Janet Durbin
Editing by Brieanna Robertson

ISBN-13: 978-1-63495-030-5

Published by
Whimsical Publications, LLC
Florida

aCKNOWLeDGeMeNT

For Science!

also BY
Darren S. Philibert

Tales from Lamplight Lane - Book 1- Squid

NOTE FOR THE READER:

Local scientist, Professor Sigmund Rubic (and no he is not the guy who invented the Rubik's Cube)* felt it necessary to deescalate the threat level of the asteroid from certain to *probable* doom. Because the only things certain in life, according to Professor Rubic, are death, taxes, and that there is unfortunately no end in sight for reality shows. However, he assures us that he is both knowledgeable and skilled enough to handle the burning ball of disaster that is about to strike the small town that he calls home—Lamplight Lane.

Erno Rubik of Hungary invented the Rubik's Cube in 1974

TABLE OF CONTENTS

1

WHEN SCIENCE AND FASHION COLLIDE

Lightning danced across a cloudy sky as rain pelted down in fat drops. Wind howled like a giant wolf baying at the moon, although no moon could be seen. A small house stood alone along the tree line of a forest that surrounded the town of Lamplight Lane. Light flashed from rectangular windows on the foundation of the house as if another smaller storm was taking place in the basement. Inside, beakers bubbled and electricity crackled in a laboratory much like the ones you see in old Frankenstein movies. The cramped lab was cluttered with all kinds of strange machines. Machines that could change the molecular structure of a man and even turn him inside-out (the latter, of course, being an unfortunate side effect). One machine, called the Retsaot (which is toaster spelled backwards) allows a person to de-toast a piece of bread in case after toasting they thought better of it and wanted to just stick to a normal slice of bread without wasting any food. There was also a section dedicated to multiple rows of cages housing a few animals. Making all the commotion was a large machine in the middle of the room that had two large spinning arms revolving around each other, turning faster and faster. Loud snaps of electric discharges and a low ominous hum emanated from the strange device. One discharge shocked a monkey (ironically named Sparky) in a cage across the room and made him scream in surprise. Sparky was upset. He stared at the man responsible for his captivity, and now his smoldering bum.

Professor Sigmund Rubic, wearing a lab coat and some strange-looking goggles, ran from one instrument panel to another, turning knobs, flipping switches, and pushing up his goggles. The machine's arms now were spinning so fast there was simply a blur of motion. Then with a loud boom, everything went quiet. The machine was still spinning, but it was as if someone reached up and poured oil all over it. Professor Rubic stopped and looked around expectantly. Nothing happened.

After powering down the machine, he walked disappointedly back to his drawing board. He didn't understand. Where had he gone wrong? He was sure it would work this time. His calculations were sound. Professor Rubic scratched his long scraggly black hair that had a stripe of white through it—from a previous experiment where he was trying to instantaneously copy any hair style from one person to another. The only test subject he had at the time was himself and a skunk nicknamed Pepe. The experiment was a complete success, except for that fact that the hairstyle was exchanged, not copied, and the effects were irreversible. Even if you shaved your head, it would always grow back the same as before. At least Professor Rubic came out with the good end of the deal while poor Pepe now has a permanent comb-over.

Professor Rubic walked into his living room and turned on the TV while plopping into his chair. The news was on, and apparently, there was some big commotion going on in the town again. A woman reporting for the local news team holding on to her jacket against the wind outside was explaining the incident. Professor Rubic turned the volume up.

"Apparently, because of a toxic spill on the freeway last week, some of the waste has seeped down into a local stream that was the main water source for a local farmer's sheep. After drinking this polluted water, the sheep were mutated into bloodthirsty, fluffy killing machines. They escaped their holding pin and terrorized the town. Amazingly, a strange void of some sort appeared just behind the rogue flock in town square and sucked them into it, saving the town in a most unusual way."

The camera panned over to show the event horizon of a wormhole, swirling and churning in a beautiful array of blue and green.

Professor Rubic jumped up off his chair. "It *did* work!"

2

STATUE OF LIMITATIONS

Francis was getting impatient. He knocked and knocked, but there was no answer at Professor Rubic's house. Clyde, Ralf, and Palyn were starting to grow bored after sitting there for fifteen minutes.

"Maybe he's sleeping and we shouldn't wake him," said Ralf.

"At 1:13 in the afternoon?" said Francis. "No, I'm sure he's down in his basement, so focused on something that he hasn't heard me knocking yet." Francis was eager to pick up Professor Rubic's latest invention. He'd promised that it was ready for use and he could pick it up today.

"Come on, Francis, I've had my limit of mosquitoes now. I'm getting eaten alive out here!" said Clyde.

"Then just change into a statue or something so they can't bite you."

"Hey, ya, that's a good idea."

Just then, the door swung open and Professor Rubic looked out. "Oh, Francis, I'm very busy today. What can I do for you?"

"You said I could pick up the device today, remember?"

"Ohhh right right right. I'm sorry, I got lost in some other project. Yes, of course, come in, come in. Wait a minute, why is the Statue of Liberty in my front yard?"

"Oh that's just Clyde...it's because of the mosquitoes," said Francis.

Professor Rubic looked at the statue, then to Francis and the others, and just shook his head as if to say, *I'm probably better off just not knowing.*

3

TO SMELL WHAT NO MAN HAS SMELLED BEFORE

Professor Rubic placed in Francis' hands a strange-looking pair of glasses. They had binocular-style lenses along with a digital band that wrapped around the head, and a pair of tubes that came off the bridge of the glasses and rounded upward so as to fit into one's nostrils.

"I give you the Smellnoculars!" said Rubic. "Anything you look at will be processed by image recognition software and then matched up in an immense database. Based on that object, a synthetic odor with be produced through the nostril outputs. You will be able to smell anything you look at, no matter how far away it is. Just be careful what you look at, because there are some things out there you really don't want to smell. Trust me. I never saw the sewage truck until it was too late." Rubic had a blank stare, as if reliving a horrible memory. He quickly snapped out of it. "Anyways, I have much work to do, boys, so off with ya now; have fun with the Smellnoculars."

Just then a large rush of wind came through the house. A ball of light formed in the middle of Rubic's living room. It grew until it was the size of either a very tall midget or a very short giant, which is to say about average height. The light disappeared, and standing there with smoke lifting from him was a man identical to Professor Rubic.

4

ALLOW MYSELF TO INTRODUCE MYSELF

Everyone stood there in amazement watching the other Rubic pace frantically around the room, talking about disaster and calculations until he stopped, just now noticing the others were there. He was staring at the boys. "Where am I?" he asked.

"Well," said Francis slowly. "You're in your house, here in Lamplight Lane."

"No, no, no, I mean where is the other me?" The original Rubic cleared his throat.

"You're...uh, I mean, I am over here."

The new Rubic turned around on his heels. "Ah, there I am." He walked over to the original Rubic and placed his hands on his shoulders. "In exactly six months, four days, nine hours, and thirty three seconds, you will destroy the world, and I'm here to stop you...ur...I mean, me."

Everyone sat down and the future Rubic began to explain the chain of events that would ultimately destroy the world six months from now.

And it goes like so...

5

IT'S THE END OF THE WORLD AS WE KNOW IT, AND I FEEL SICK

"Approximately two weeks before the world is destroyed, I discovered an asteroid hurtling toward Earth. I brought this news to the attention of city hall. I assured them that I was researching the disaster and felt confident that I would produce a solution. I had come a long way with the wormhole machine I called the Wormholer. Yes, I know, it's not very original, but I'm a scientist, not a maker-up-of-names person...you know what I mean. So with hours upon hours of calculations and tests, including one where my projections were just slightly off and I accidentally created a wormhole in the middle of Jolly Roger's ice cream truck transporting it to who knows where, I finally perfected it, or so I thought. I approached the city council once again. I told them I had developed a machine that could create a wormhole large enough to surround the entire town, thus transporting it temporarily into orbit and out of the path of the asteroid, then once it had struck, we could simply transport the town back. I also explained that the wormhole would encase our atmosphere like a sealed dome so there would be plenty of air. They asked if it would even matter if the town was moved out of the way—wouldn't the asteroid just destroy Earth when it struck? But I assured them that this was a smallish asteroid and when it hit it would just make a huge smoking crater where the town used to be; it was not large enough to affect the Earth in any cataclysmic way. They were overjoyed at the prospect of this solution and commissioned me to begin preparations immediately, for the asteroid would be there within twenty-four hours. I had everything ready to go within twenty-two hours from then. I checked my calculations and double-checked them. It was time to transport the town out of harm's way.

"Everyone had gathered in town square, where I positioned the Wormholer. I powered it up and activated it. Its arms spun at an incredible speed and then it emitted a pulse that started to form a wormhole up in the sky above the town. It grew larger and larger until it spanned the entire length of the town. When it was at full capacity, I brought the wormhole down over top the city. It passed through all of us and the town. Someone puked. It wasn't because of the wormhole, well not directly anyways. The wind from the wormhole passing through blew off Palyn's bag and some unfortunate person was staring right at him. But other than that, it went fine, or so we all had thought. We looked up in the sky and the asteroid was almost upon us. After some simple calculations, I told the rest of the town not to worry, that the asteroid was now miles off course and it would not hit us. We were as planned, safely in orbit and out of the way. The entire town, now curious to watch the impact on the Earth, went to the edge of town for the spectacular view. Within the hour, we saw the asteroid fly by on its way to Earth. We all waited patiently. I told them that we should see the impact anytime now. Then we saw a tiny puff of what looked like smoke. Then, about thirty seconds after that, we all watched in horror as the Earth exploded in a ball of flame, the shock wave jostling us and knocking most people off their feet. Someone puked. Palyn had lost his bag again.

6

WOrMHOLes IN a NUTSHeLL

I would now like to take the opportunity to explain how wormhole physics works by using the following wormhole metrics.

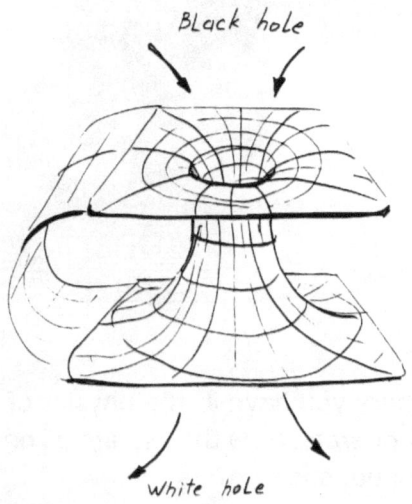

wormholes

$$ds^2 = -\left(1 - \frac{2M(r)}{r}\right)dt^2 + \left(1 - \frac{2M(r)}{r}\right)^{-1}dr^2 + r^2 d\Omega^2$$

$\theta = \pi/2$ schwarzschild solution
$t = constant$

$$ds^2 = -c^2 dt^2 + dL^2 + (k^2 + L^2)(d\theta^2 + \sin^2\theta\, d\varphi^2)$$

$$ds^2 = -c^2\left(1 - \frac{2GM}{rc^2}\right)dt^2 + \frac{dr^2}{1 - \frac{2GM}{rc^2}} + r^2(d\theta^2 + \sin^2\theta\, d\varphi^2)$$

$$u^2 - v^2 = \left(\frac{r}{2M} - 1\right)e^{r/2M}$$

$$\frac{v}{u} = \begin{cases} \coth\frac{t}{4M} \\ 1 \\ \tanh\frac{t}{4M} \end{cases} \quad for\ r \begin{cases} < 2M \\ = 2M \\ > 2M \end{cases}$$

$$ds^2 = \frac{32\,M^3}{r}e^{-r/2M}(-du^2 + du^2) + r^2 d\Omega^2$$

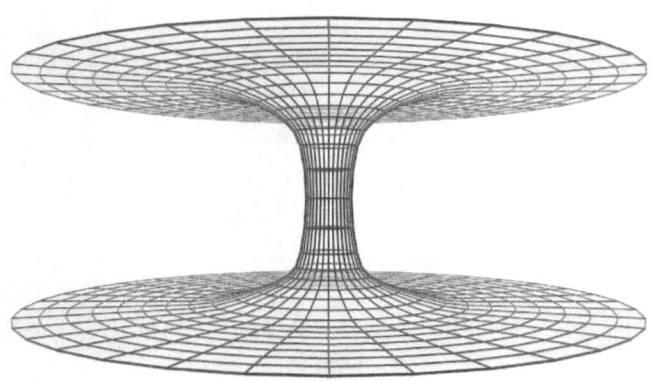

So, there you have it, the physics of wormholes and how they operate. Now that we are all on the same page, let's continue, shall we?

7

COFFee: THe CaUSe OF aND SOLUTION TO aLL OF eaRTH'S PROBLeMS

After the future Rubic was through explaining the up-coming disaster, he proceeded to explain what it was that caused the explosion and the solution to preventing it. What happened was that, somewhere in the calcula-tions, he created the wormhole slightly too big, thus cre-ating a fissure to open in the cavity where the town once was. When the asteroid hit, the open fissure caused a chain reaction all the way to the Earth's core. Now that the cause had been identified, Professor Rubic had stud-ied, analyzed, and calculated his way to the most minute detail, and after weeks of non-stop research, finally came up with the answer. Coffee.

During the exhausting week prior to the asteroid's arrival, Professor Rubic had gone to the local store to buy his favorite brand of coffee. But to the Professor's disap-pointment, they did not get the shipment of coffee that he preferred. So a disgruntled Rubic settled for an inferi-or substitute, and that, in and of itself, was the problem, for the second-rate coffee hadn't given him the waking edge needed to make the proper calculations—he later went to city hall and started a petition to have a Star-bucks Coffee shop built in town.

He chuckled inwardly when thinking back to that day at the store. He had said to himself, "Just get the generic brand, it's not the end of the world." So, upon investigating further, he realized why the store had not gotten his favorite brand of coffee in that week. The warehouse supervisor who had filled out the order sheet had indeed written a six in the quantity line, but because of bad hand writing, the six ended up looking like a zero, and so nothing was ordered.

Rubic now had the answer to fixing this whole mess. They must go back to when the warehouse supervisor was in elementary school and help him practice his penmanship, so that in the future, his six will not look like a zero, the coffee would be ordered, and thus the world saved.

8

aTTacK ON THe CLONeS

Everyone was now in the basement laboratory getting things prepared for their journey. The future Rubic wanted to bring along the present Rubic so there would be another brilliant mind there to double check calculations. Also, the Professors decided that the boys, with their strange but sometimes useful abilities, could come in handy. The boys excitedly agreed to come along.

Just then a loud ruckus occurred. Everyone one heard an "Oops" followed by a repeated thudding sound. They looked up to see a tubby figure rolling down the stairs directly at them. The future Rubic and the boys all jumped out of the way in time, but unfortunately for the present Rubic, he was rammed into by the tubby figure and propelled into a high voltage transformer. The present Rubic twitched as ten thousand volts of electricity pulsed through his body. A moment later, all that was left of the present Rubic was a smoldering pile of black ash on the floor. The boys stared in shock with horrified faces. Then, just over to their right, a boxy-looking machine switched on and started to hum and rattle. After a few seconds, there was a ding like that on a microwave and a door opened on the front. Professor Rubic stepped out.

**As his occupation of scientist transitioned from esteemed to insanely brilliant, and after an almost fatal accident, Professor Rubic decided it would be a good idea to build a cloning machine along with a dead man switch so if any unforeseeable and fatal mistake was made, the machine would be activated and a cloned Rubic would emerge along with up-to-date memory imprint.

After explaining this to the amazed kids, he walked over to a rack of dozens of identical-looking devices. The dead man switches. He grabbed one, strapped it around his waist, and activated it. He turned and stared at the chubby boy who was looking very abashed and chewing on his bottom lip like it was a piece of beef jerky.

Thaddeus "Waddles" Fedora.

He was an acquaintance of the boys, albeit a slight bit annoying. They called him by his nickname Waddles because if you had met him and seen him walk, you would come to the conclusion as well that he more waddled like a penguin than walked. He was also born with Cacophobia (a fear of ugliness) which soon became Catoptrophobia (a fear of mirrors). Waddles was the most accident prone person in the world, and that was not an exaggeration. He was actually nominated by The Guinness Book of World Records for most accident prone. When meeting with the judges for The Guinness Book, he had the award in the bag before he even entered the building. When exiting the minivan, his shirt was promptly caught in the automatic closing door. Not noticing this, his mother then sped away, dragging Waddles along for a few feet before his shirt ripped. After tumbling into oncoming traffic, he caused a massive pile-up that overturned a semi-truck full of eggs, a vegetable truck, and a cart selling sliced meats. While waiting inside for the judges, he got tangled in the longest armpit hair, tripped over the longest toenails, and was sat on by the world's fattest albino. On this, the hottest day of the year too, Waddles took home two awards, one for the most accident prone and another for largest omelet.

"So, whatcha doin'?" asked Waddles

"Sorry, Waddles, we don't have time to hang out today, we are about to leave on an important mission to save the world," said Francis.

"Oh cool, can I come?"

"No, Waddles, not this time, we really have to go. It's of the utmost importance..." Before Francis was halfway through his sentence, Waddles was already distracted by a shiny orb to his left and was thoroughly poking it with his finger.

The crew, with two Professor Rubics and the four boys, were all ready. They gathered together in the middle of the room as per the instructions from the future Rubic. He prepared his time traveling device by typing in some sequence, asked everyone if they were ready and if they had gone to the bathroom before they left. Not that the trip would take long and they might have to go to the bathroom, but because of the time travel effects on the body, there was a slight probability that a full bladder could explode.

As Waddles was playing with the shiny orb, he caught a glimpse of his reflection in its mirror shine and screamed something awful. Turning and running away from it, he ran straight into the group as they disappeared into the space-time continuum.

9

SHOCKING DEVELOPMENTS

Arriving twenty-five years into the past, the group materialized behind Lamplight Elementary School. Waddles' carried momentum launched him into a briar patch. "Ah, perfectly accurate," said the future Rubic, taking in their surroundings and then looking at his time device. "Gotta love science!"

Clyde turned to Francis. "Oh great, Waddles came through with us. Someone's gotta keep an eye on him or he'll step on a squirrel or something, and when we get back, apes will rule the world."

"I agree, so here is what you need to do. If Waddles starts to wander off, just turn into something shiny and that should wrangle him back," said Francis. Clyde nodded in agreement.

The future Rubic proceeded to explain that the target's name was Oscar Vint. Young Oscar was currently attending Lamplight Elementary and would be found within. All they had to do was simply wait until after school was out then follow him home. After they found out where he lived, Professor Rubic would then show up and claim to be a tutor that was assigned to young Oscar to help with his studies. After a few short lessons in math, geography, and quantum physics (at least Professor Rubic hoped they would have time to cover that), he would then crack the whip on his penmanship.

Waddles started to follow a bullfrog he saw hopping by.

Clyde's head turned into a disco ball.

As they waited across the street at local bookstore called Reading by Lamplight, they heard the school bell ring and the children started spilling out of the school. Future Rubic produced a picture of young Oscar from his pocket that he had collected earlier, along with the rest of the info on Oscar back when calculating the solution to the whole Earth-blowing-up problem. They spotted Oscar and proceeded to shadow him home.

Waddles was captivated by a large moth on the side of a building.

Clyde's arm turned into a large sparkler, attracting both Waddles and the moth.

On the way to Oscar's house, they passed the town's power station. The future Rubic made some comment about how primitive it was compared to his electricity conductors in his basement. Then they watched as Oscar stopped at the chain link fence surrounding the electricity station and was apparently looking at something. Within the fenced off section there was a cat that was lazily reclining on the grass. Oscar knelt down and began to call the cat over to him. The cat gave him the usual "why should I waste my time on you" look, and glanced away as if bored by his beckoning. The others were across the street behind the town's tall water tower that had "Welcome to Lamplight Lane" written on it, waiting for Oscar to continue on his way home. Straining to see what Oscar was looking at, Clyde forgot his responsibility to look after Waddles.

Seeing something interesting in a store window just a

few feet away, he wandered over to take a look. It was the most amazing-looking coin collection he had ever seen, very shiny. Looking from one thing to another in the window, he came suddenly to a small mirror. The group jumped as they heard a scream and saw Waddles running (rather waddling fast) towards them. As they moved out of the way, Waddles ran smack into one of the legs of the water tower. He hit with a loud *crack*! He fell to the ground with a thud. Slowly at first, then building more rapidly, there was a sound like the splintering of wood. Ending with a last horrible crack, the leg broke, followed by the other three legs. The entire water tower toppled forward right towards little Oscar.

The huge tower came down with powerful crash and fell just a few feet short of Oscar. The tower exploded, blasting Oscar with tons of water against the fence. The water splashed past him and onto the power station's multiple transformers, erupting in an explosion of sparks. Oscar shook and jolted from a slight blow-off of the electric discharge. The cat, however, was not so fortunate. For we all know that wet cat and electricity do not get along so well. After the smoke cleared, the group watched as Oscar got up, dusted himself off, and walked shakily towards his house. They all turned and looked at Waddles with faces that said two things.

1. You have got to be kidding me.

2. Well, it's not like I didn't see that coming.

"Oops," said Waddles as he giggled nervously. They all continued to stare at him. "Oh come on like you didn't see that coming?"

They arrived at Oscar's house and watched him walk up his front steps, ring the doorbell, and then collapse on the porch, smoke rising from his hair. His mother came to the door and, with a yell to Oscar's father, they called 911 and an ambulance came and rushed poor Oscar to the hospital.

10

WHEN PIGS KICK

The Rubics and the boys shadowed Oscar to the hospital and were relieved when he was released later that day to go back home. Apparently, there were just minor burns and mild concussion. They decided it would be best to wait a few days before trying the whole plan again to give Oscar some time to rest up and heal. They checked into the local motel called The Lamplight Inn. The next two days were fairly uneventful except for the following:

Day 1
7:00 a.m.: Waddles woke everyone up because he got turned around in his sleeping bag and couldn't find the way out.
7:02 a.m.: Waddles fell out of the bed and promptly got lost in the sleeping bag once again.
8:00 a.m.: The group had breakfast at the local diner called The Lamplight Special.
8:12 a.m.: Waddles simultaneously squirted grapefruit juice in Clyde's eye and stuck his straw up his nose when missing it with his mouth.
9:40 a.m.: The group decided to roam around town,

testing out the Smellnoculars.

9:45 a.m.: Clyde smelled some flowers from four blocks away.

9:50 a.m.: Ralf smelled a pie that was cooling on a window sill half a mile away.

10:00 a.m.: Palyn smelled nothing because of his rice bag over his face.

10:02 a.m.: Waddles got the goggles turned upside down and poked both his eyes with the nostril tubes.

12:00 p.m.: The group decided to have a picnic by the old pond, and Ralf had them entertained with frog acrobatics.

1:00 p.m. – 4:00 p.m.: Waddles tripped, fell, disappeared, reappeared, cried, screamed, puked, got poison ivy, desecrated a grave site, burned down a chicken co-op, broke five windows, caused a landslide, got stuck in a minivan door, made two other people puke, got kicked by a pig (no one even knew pigs could kick until today), fell down a well, got trampled by a moose, and started a feud between two families.

5:00 p.m.: The group passed by old man Groy's house and saw the storyteller on the porch rocking in his chair; he looked exactly the same as twenty-five years from now.

6:00 p.m.: The Rubics took a sneak peek at their past self working in the lab.

6:05 p.m.: Waddles leaned on an old tree that fell over and crashed through the basement window, causing a malfunction in a new laser machine Rubic was working on that almost killed him, thus leading him to start immediately on the cloning machine and the dead man switch.

7:00 p.m.: Clyde turned into a roller coaster for everyone's amusement.

7:05 p.m.: Waddles fell out.

9:00 p.m.: They return to the hotel for the night.

10:00 p.m.: Waddles got lost in his sleeping bag again. 10:01 pm: No one was surprised and they turned out the lights.

Day 2
6:32 a.m.: Rubic couldn't sleep and started tampering with his time device.

Day 3

7:00 a.m.: Everyone was shocked when yesterday it was the 20th and today, after waking, it was now the 22nd, especially poor Waddles, whose birthday was on the 21st and was going to have to repeat the fifth grade

Now it was time to review the plan with the group and make preparations. Soon, three p.m. came and they were off to Oscar's house.

11

IPOD MATERIAL

Mrs. Vint opened her front door to a lanky-looking gentleman with black scraggly hair and a white stripe down the middle. "Morning, madam, my name is Heinrich Cube. Lamplight Elementary has sent me as a tutor to assist your young Oscar in his studies. Is he home today?"

"Yes, he is home, but I'm sure there has been some sort of mistake," said Mrs. Vint. "Our Oscar has been bringing home A's on all his assignments and also aced a pop quiz yesterday. It seems that ever since his little accident three days ago, he's become a little Einstein. So I really don't think he needs a tutor."

Professor Rub...er, uh, Heinrich Cube had a very curious look on his face. "And his penmanship...it's...legible?"

"Oh yes, it's very beautiful. It's even better than mine!" exclaimed Mrs. Vint.

"I see," said Heinrich. "Very well then, if you say so, I'll take your word for it." Heinrich turned to leave then quickly turned around. "So if Oscar was to write the number six, you could easily distinguish it from a zero right?"

"Definitely, the curvature is simply splendid. There would be no mistaking his sixes for zeros," assured Mrs. Vint.

"What if his right hand was bound, would you be able to read a six written by his left hand?"

"His left hand penmanship is even better than his right," said Mrs. Vint. Heinrich furrowed his brow in thought and rubbed his chin. "What if he was bound hand and foot, and hung upside down from a rope, while suspended above a tank of piranhas with his mouth glued shut and had only mechanical pencil lead stuck in his nostril and a leprechaun was dancing on—"

"Mr. Cube," interrupted Mrs. Vint, "his penmanship is superb, I assure you" Heinrich Cube cleared his throat. "Uh, yes, yes, understood. Thank you for your time today, Mrs. Vint, and have a wonderful day." The door shut.

Professor Rubic joined the others who had been hiding around the corner. He explained that the accident with the water tower and electricity had somehow jump-started young Oscar's brain. Now he was the perfect pupil, and his penmanship even rivaled that of Gertrude Wineschladts*. Everyone was ecstatic and amazed at the outcome. They all clapped. Waddles missed and slapped himself in the face.

*Gertrude Wineschladt: Gold medalist of the IPOD (International Penmanship Olympics Decathlon) from 2004-2008 (...duh)

12

Back to the New Future's Past

With their job done (hopefully), the Rubics decided it was time to travel back to the present and see if indeed they had averted disaster. The future Rubic inputted some calculations into his time device and, after checking to make sure no one had to go to the bathroom, the group was swallowed in a ball of light and whisked away.

A moment later, they were standing at the edge of the forest looking down upon Earth. They were in the town when it was in orbit still.

"So are we back to just before the asteroid hit?" asked Ralf.

"Yes and no," answered the future Rubic. "The town has not left the Earth yet."

"Then how are we here up in orbit right now?" asked Francis

"Well, I guess I should explain other events that happened before I came back to the past," the future Rubic began.

No more than a day after the town watched the Earth explode, the town council met and started to organize a new world order, since the town of Lamplight Lane was now all that was left of Earth. The mayor quickly nominated himself as the President of Earth. Soon, property lines became country borders. Problems began when different countries started implementing their own foreign currency and every country claimed that their money was worth more than all the others. Inflation skyrocketed. Except for the ongoing war between two rival families that started twenty-five years ago, wars now broke out between countries (which basically was two families hunkered down behind porches or shrubs throwing rocks and stink bombs at each other until one house was so utterly trashed it was condemned and the family evicted). After months of this, the town was in sad sorts. When Professor Rubic had finished his time device, he felt so bad for his town and the mess it was in he traveled back to before the wars got bad and then brought the entire town back, to before the town's extraction into orbit, with him. He couldn't bear the fact that when he would change the past, this future Lamplight would cease to exist. He would be saving them from non-existence and give them a second chance to institute a form government that would work.

With that said, the group stood there, watching the beauty of the Earth hanging upon nothing. Professor Rubic said that soon they should see the town appear in orbit a few miles off from their current location. They would simply wait for the asteroid to pass them and hope that after the strike, the Earth would still be there. While they waited, more and more town people came to the edge to watch the event, including the future Francis, Clyde, Ralf, and Payln. They were beside themselves with excitement (literally). Professor Rubic then announced that the other Lamplight had now just appeared a few miles off and could barely be seen in the distance. Not long after that, they saw the asteroid barreling down upon the Earth. Everyone waited, holding their breath. They saw the impact. Then there was an explosion...

13

everything's Better with Pirates

...of cheers as the Earth stayed intact. People were hugging and yelling and incredibly happy for the past versions of themselves. Oh, and the rest of the Earth too. They watched as the tiny speck that was the other Lamplight Lane disappeared back down to Earth. The mission had been successful.

That night, all dressed up like pirates and had a celebratory town barbeque, and fun was had by all.* The boys had fun learning about things from a few months in the future from their future selves. The Rubics got busy comparing notes and ideas. Waddles fell into the town well, finding the future Waddles already there. They also saw old man Groys. He came wobbling up to them. "Hello there, boys, this sure is an amazing night. Say, that reminds me, did I ever tell you about the time an asteroid destroyed the Earth?"

They all looked at each other.

"Ya, Groys," said Francis. "I think we remember that one."

After a while, the boys came up to the Rubics going over notes for a new device that would beam the juice directly out of fruits so as to avoid getting squirted in the eye when doing it manually. Francis mentioned to the Rubics that they should go find Oscar and congratulate him on a job well done, and that he played a major role in both destroying and saving the Earth. The Rubics agreed and set off with the boys to the Lamplight Lane back on Earth to see him.

They arrived at the local market where Oscar was employed and asked the store clerk if they could talk to the warehouse manager. He pointed them out to the warehouse. They came up to a woman sitting behind a desk and asked her if they could speak with the warehouse manager.

*The day the earth was saved was Sept 19th, which is also National Talk like a Pirate Day, so the town decided to have a combined celebration, honoring the two.

She looked at them with a smile. "Sure, how can I help you?"

"Isn't Oscar Vint the warehouse manager here?" asked the future Rubic.

"Nope, sorry, I've never heard of an Oscar Vint, and I've been the manager here for eight years now. My name is Emily."

They all stared at her, wondering what could have become of Oscar Vint. "Can I help you with something, though?" she asked.

"Oh, no, sorry, we must have the wrong warehouse. Thank you, though," stuttered Rubic. She smiled and they turned and left. The future Rubic exhaled and told them that after this long trip, he was ready for a vacation. The past Rubic agreed and said it was probably time for the future Rubic to take them back home to the Lamplight Lane back on Earth. They all vanished in a ball of light. A moment later, they came back for Waddles who had somehow managed to be left behind on the first attempt.

Emily went back to her paperwork after the group left. On the order form for next week's shipment, she put down a six for quantity next to Rubic's favorite coffee. The six was nicely written. She was no Gertrude Wineschladt, but it was good enough.

14

TIME IS LIKE A MYSTERY TOPPED WITH AN ENIGMA, DIPPED IN A PARADOX AND SERVED WITH A SIDE OF IMPROBABILITY

-Two weeks ago

At the National Aeronautics and Space Administration, men in lab coats and pocket protectors busily ran around a large room with TV consoles and computers with highly sophisticated algorithms displayed on them. They were about to launch a new operation on Mars that would open a part of a crater believed to have water crystals inside. The demolitions crew gave the green light. The lead scientist stood at the top of the complex looking at a huge TV monitor displaying an unmanned robot that he designed, about to arm the explosive. He gave his calculations to a member of the senior staff to enter into a computer terminal. After entering the formula, it initiated the robot to detonate. The explosion was much bigger than expected. As a result, a huge piece of Martian rock broke off and hurtled into space, on a crash course with Earth. All the scientists' jaws hit the floor. The senior scientist came back to the lead scientist, who had handed him the calculations to input. "I'm sorry, Oscar. I input the wrong number. I thought your seven was a nine."

aBOUT THe aUTHOr

Darren S. Philibert

Darren Shawn Philibert has loved fantasy and adventure stories ever since his grandmother bought him the Chronicles of Narnia series by C.S Lewis when in middle school. His hobbies include reading (duh) board games and binge watching sci-fi shows. He lives in Eugene, Oregon with his book-loving wife Tara and their dorky cat Stormageddon (Stormy for short)